This **Chicken House** book belongs to:

....

....

....

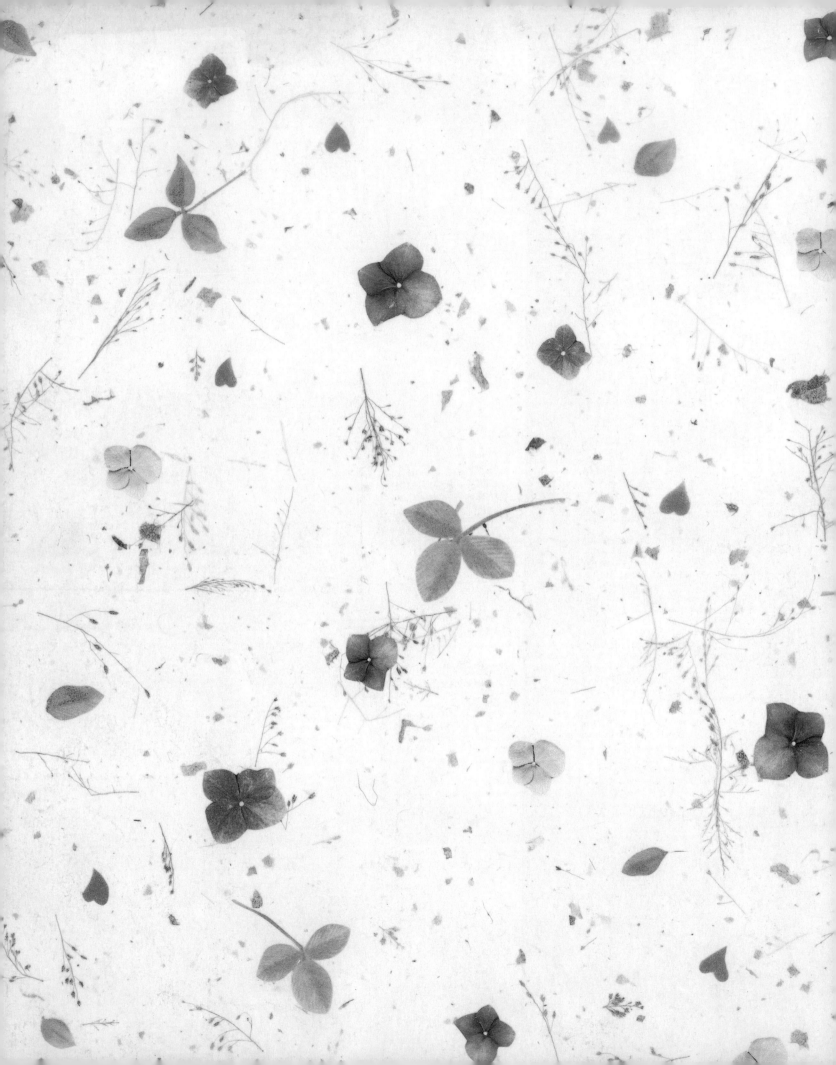

With hoppiness and love to all the
bunny valentines out there. MM

To Ollie and Phoebe –CJC

© 2006 The Chicken House

First published in the United Kingdom in 2006 by
The Chicken House, 2 Palmer Street, Frome, Somerset, BA11 1DS
www.doublecluck.com
This paperback edition first published in 2007

Text © 2006 Michaela Morgan
Illustrations © 2006 Caroline Jayne Church

Designed by Ian Butterworth

Printed and bound in China for Imago
1 3 5 7 9 10 8 6 4 2

British Library Cataloguing in Publication Data available
Library of Congress Cataloguing in Publication data available

ISBN 978-1-904442-97-4

Dear Bunny

Michaela Morgan

Illustrated by
Caroline Jayne Church

Chicken House

Once upon a time there were two bunny rabbits.
Their names were Valentino and Valenteeny —
or Tino and Teeny for short.

One lived here

And one lived there

Every now and then they would
peep at each other and think,

Oh, how lovely that bunny is!

But neither of them said a
thing because they were both
very, very, very, very,
very, very (very) shy.

One day Tino had an idea.

I'll write a little letter — just a friendly hello
sort of letter — and I'll put it in the hollow log
for Teeny to find.

This is the letter Tino wrote:

Dear Teeny Bunny

I hope you are well.

I thought I would write you a letter because it's such a lovely warm day over here. There is some of the sweetest, most tender clover I have ever seen. It is PERFECT.

Perhaps you would like to hop over and share some of the warmth and sunshine and clover with me?

I look forward very much to hearing from you.

Best wishes
Tino

Then Tino went hop hop hopping
over to the hollow log and popped in the letter,
just as it started to rain.

A little later, Teeny had just the same idea
and so set off with a fine present of leaves
and petals and a little note for Tino.

Teeny popped everything into the hollow
log and hopped off quickly as the
rain plip plopped down.

It's getting
wetter!

Quick!
Back to the
nest!

This is the note Teeny wrote:

Dear Tino

I hope you will like these lovely leaves and petals. They are very beautiful and so very sweet and tender. They have **exceptional** tenderness. I picked them specially for you. Please accept them as a small gift from me.

Teeny

PS I so look forward to hearing from you.

Meanwhile, by the river bank, the mouse family and their nest were getting wetter and wetter and wetter.

Plip
plop
pitter
patter
SPERLOSH!

'Ugh' went Mrs Mouse.
'Brrr' went Mr Mouse.
And
'WAAAAAA.
went all the babies.

Through the rain they scrambled,
looking for shelter.

And where do you think they went?

To the hollow log!

It was dry and warm and snugly lined with
paper, petals and leaves.
Perfect!

Soon they were all busy
nibbling and gnawing and
shredding for bedding and
ripping and weaving and
making the cosiest nest you
could ever imagine,
complete with beautiful
petal blankets.

All through the long and stormy days,
the mice snoozed. They were snug and safe
and surrounded by Love, Warmth and
Exceptional Tenderness.

exceptional

some of the sweetest,

tenderness.

PERFECT.

and

sunshin

are very beautiful and

At last, the sun peeped through the clouds
and the mice peeped out of their nest.

And what do you think they saw?

Sob, sob, sob,
no letter for me!

Oh dear!

What have
we done?

Oh, oh, oh!

And then a little later . . .

'Oh,'
squeaked Mrs Mouse.
'Oh, oh, oh!'
'What have we done?'
squeaked Mr Mouse.
'What can we do?'
squeaked the babies.

Then for very small creatures they had a very

big

idea.

tenderness.

sweetest,

They decided to give up
their nest, put the words back
together and make a message for
the lovelorn bunnies. They would
only choose the best words,
the ones that had kept them
warmest through the
cold and stormy
days.

Specially for you.

most tender

Best wishes

Specially for you

hope warm wishes and

for the sweetest Best

you are

so

oh so very

Please

sunshiney thoughts

most tender love

so lovely

beautiful

exceptionally sweet

and PERFECT

accept

me

Tino hopped along and gazed at it.

Specially for you

hope warm wishes and

for the sweetest Best

you are

so

Oh so very

Pleas

Teeny hopped along and gazed at it.

sunshiney thoughts

most tender love

so lovely

beautiful

xceptionally sw

and PERFECT

accept

me

Then they gazed
at each other
and that was that . . .

...they both lived

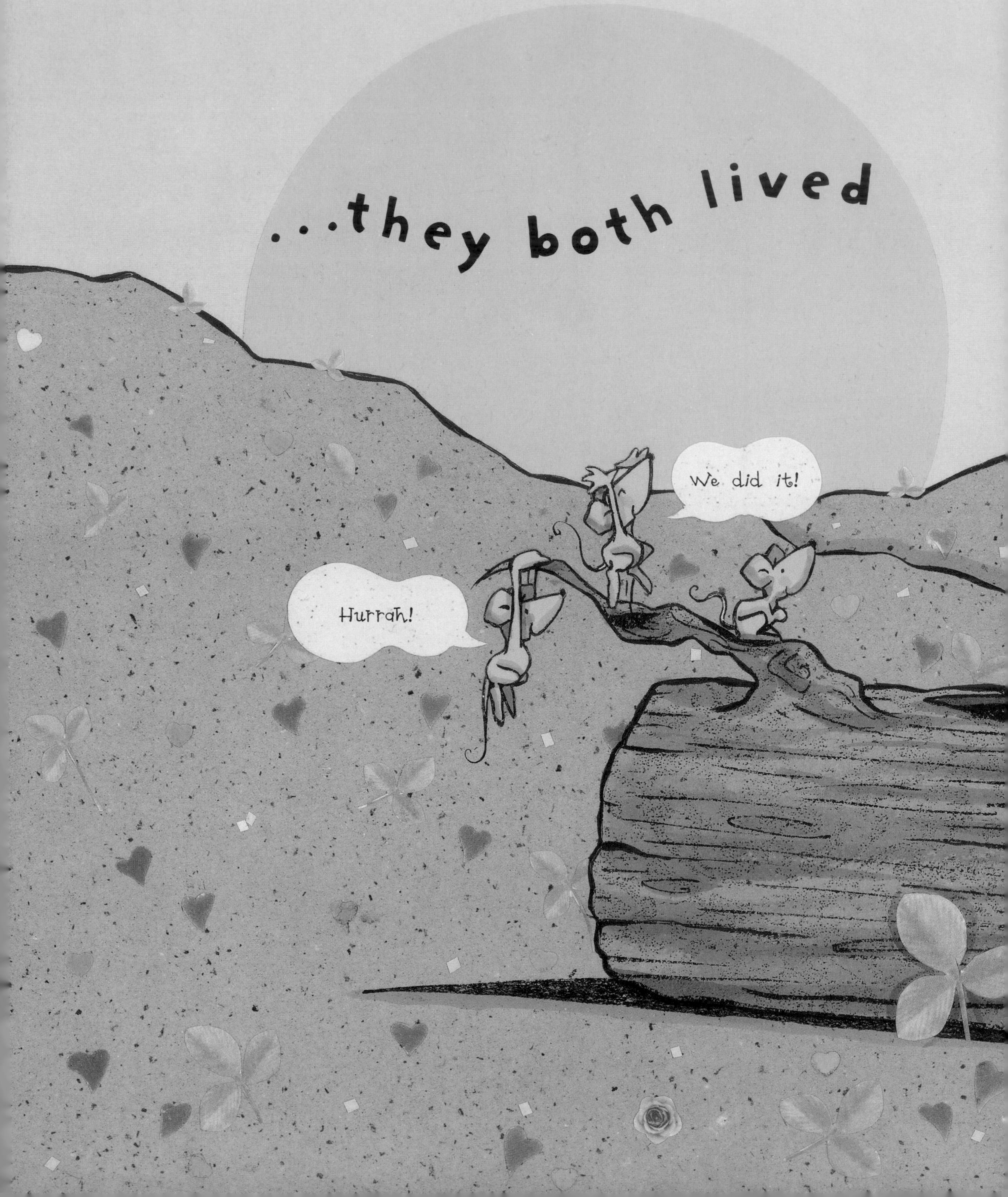

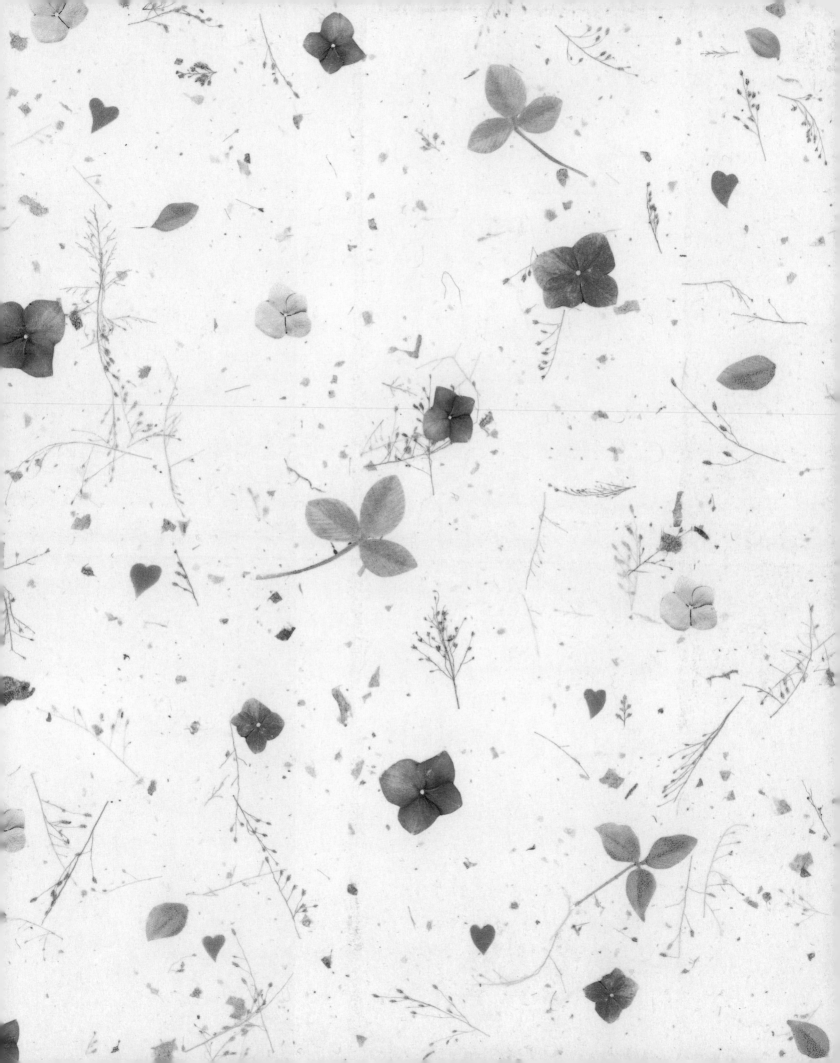